Disney
Tangled

A Dazzling Day

ADAPTED BY DEVIN ANN WOOSTER

ILLUSTRATED BY BRITTNEY LEE
DESIGNED BY STUART SMITH

A Random House PICTUREBACK® Book

Random House 🏠 New York

Library of Congress Control Number: 2010923934
ISBN: 978-0-7364-2721-0
www.randomhouse.com/kids
Printed in the United States of America
10 9 8 7 6 5 4 3 2 1

Long ago and far away, there lived a beautiful young woman named Rapunzel. She had a special gift: seventy feet of magical hair. She had never, ever been outside the tower where Mother Gothel kept her hidden away.

Every year on her birthday, Rapunzel gazed out her tower window at the sparkling lights that rose into the nighttime sky. The lights were meant for her—she was certain of it. And Rapunzel yearned to leave the tower, just once, to see those s p a r k l i n g l i g h t s . . . .

On the day before her eighteenth birthday, Rapunzel was wondering how to find the source of the lights. Suddenly, a thief named Flynn climbed into her window. Flynn was trying to escape from the royal guard, who were determined to catch him.

Pascal, Rapunzel's chameleon friend, agreed that Flynn did not look like the ruffians Mother Gothel had warned her about. So Rapunzel asked Flynn to guide her to the floating lights. Flynn agreed!

The next day, Rapunzel's heart fluttered as they neared the kingdom where the lights would be launched that night. She was so close—until Maximus, a horse from the royal guard, appeared. Maximus had finally hunted Flynn down and wanted to put him in jail. But Rapunzel convinced him to let Flynn go for just one day.

Just then, a lovely chiming sound floated through the air. . . .

Following the sound, Rapunzel raced up
a small hill and saw the kingdom!

The chimes came from the kingdom's bells,
ringing in the new day. Below the palace's
peaked towers stood a village filled with
thatched-roofed houses and inviting shops.
Rapunzel felt more excited than ever.

Rapunzel was amazed by everything she saw in the village.
People were talking happily, hanging out their laundry, and
selling and buying things. They were all preparing for that
night's launching of the

floating lanterns.

Rapunzel gasped in delight as she rushed to see more, but something *pulled* her hair.

People were accidentally stepping on all **seventy feet** of it!

Some little girls were braiding one another's hair nearby. When they saw Rapunzel approaching, their eyes lit up with delight. They had never braided such long hair before! When they were finished, Rapunzel walked away with a neat braid bundled down her back.

Nothing could stop Rapunzel now! She just had to wait until
nightfall for the lights to appear. In the meantime, she found
lots of new things to do in the kingdom! In a village shop, she
tried on a beautiful dress.

Rapunzel shared pretty pink pastries with Flynn. She loved the way the sweet frosting glazed her lips and tickled her taste buds. She had never eaten anything this **marvelous** in her entire life.

Rapunzel found a bookstore and explored every shelf. She **pulled books down** to the floor and studied them with Flynn. She eagerly read adventure stories and saw pictures of foreign lands—all sorts of things she had never known about.

Rapunzel found people who were drawing beautiful, colorful pictures on the streets. Happily, she joined right in. She liked **everyone** she met!

"It is time, good people! Gather around! Yes, yes! Gather around!" A town crier was calling out to everyone. "Today, we dance to celebrate our lost princess. It is a dance of hope, in which partners start together, separate, and return to one another—just as our princess will return to us one day."

But as the man spoke, Rapunzel found herself standing in front of a large mosaic of the King and the Queen holding their baby. Something stirred deep inside Rapunzel as her green eyes met the identical green eyes of the Princess in the painting. And the Queen—why, she looked so familiar that Rapunzel's jaw dropped.

It was like looking in a **mirror!**

Soon everyone began to dance. Rapunzel and Flynn looked at each other shyly. Then they grasped hands and joined in, staring only at each other as they came together and separated among the joyous crowd.

Rapunzel felt as if she had lived a lifetime in one dazzling day. It changed the way she looked at the world.

It was beautiful and

wonderful out here!

At last, nighttime arrived. Flynn led Rapunzel to a boat and rowed away from the shore.

"What if it's not everything I dreamed it would be?" she asked.

"It will be," Flynn reassured her.

Darkness fell, and Rapunzel gazed in awe as thousands of colorful lanterns rose into the sky. It was her grandest dream come true!

Flynn reached behind him and pulled out a surprise for Rapunzel: two lanterns! Together, they launched them high into the air. Rapunzel's heart soared as the lights floated into the sky. It was the perfect end to a dazzling day. And all she could do was wonder what fantastic new discoveries were yet to come. . . .